half popped

by Jeff Feuerstein

illustrations by Dayna Brandoff and Alex Miller

Copyright © 2013 Jeffrey Feuerstein

Illustrations copyright © 2013 Dayna Brandoff and Alex Justin Miller

All rights reserved by Burger Night Publishing Partners.
Learn more at www.kennythekernel.com

No part of this book may be reproduced or transmitted in any form or by any means, electronic or mechanical, including photocopying, recording, or by any information storage and retrieval system, without prior written permission from the copyright owner, except for the inclusion of brief quotations in a review.

Published in Brooklyn, New York, United States of America

ISBN-13: 978-1492356462
ISBN-10: 1492356468
LCCN: 2013916768

FIRST EDITION

For Shel who inspired us then...and for Tess who inspires us now.
—— JRF & DRB

For Adam, Beatrice, and Michael.
The support system behind all my endeavors
—— AJM

Kenny the kernel was only half popped.
He turned out that way when the microwave stopped.

The fully popped corn filled the bowl to the brim

while the smooth,
unpopped kernels
lined the bottom with him.

In swooped a hand and
scooped up the snack.
A chew and a swallow – it
swooped in right back.

And down underneath, Kenny would wait
while all of the fully popped popcorn got ate.
There were just some slim pickings with butter and salt
as if all the gold popcorn had been swiped from a vault.

There was no more eating of kernels half-grown,
and Kenny, poor Kenny, felt very alone.

He decided to leave that
once brimming bowl
and wander the kitchen to
roll for a stroll.

Kenny opened the fridge to see what he saw...
a frowning young veggie, organic and raw.

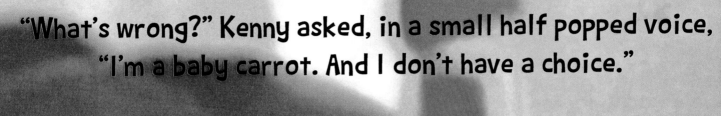

"All the carrots in here are so long and so tall
and they make fun of me for being quite small."

"Well look on the bright side," Kenny replied,
"you've got great color no matter your size.
You're healthy and crunchy and help people see!
At least you're not a half popped kernel like me."

"You're right!" said the carrot, as big as he could,
speaking just like a grown carrot would.

Kenny's journey continued
down to the fruit bin
where he heard a
boisterous squabble begin.

"I wish I was green!" – "Well I wish I was red!"
Two grapes were debating the skin on their heads.

"Oh quiet you two," Kenny let loose,
"stop all the shouting or I'll squish you to juice!

You're green and you're red, but you're both very sweet.
You make for a delicious, nutritious treat."

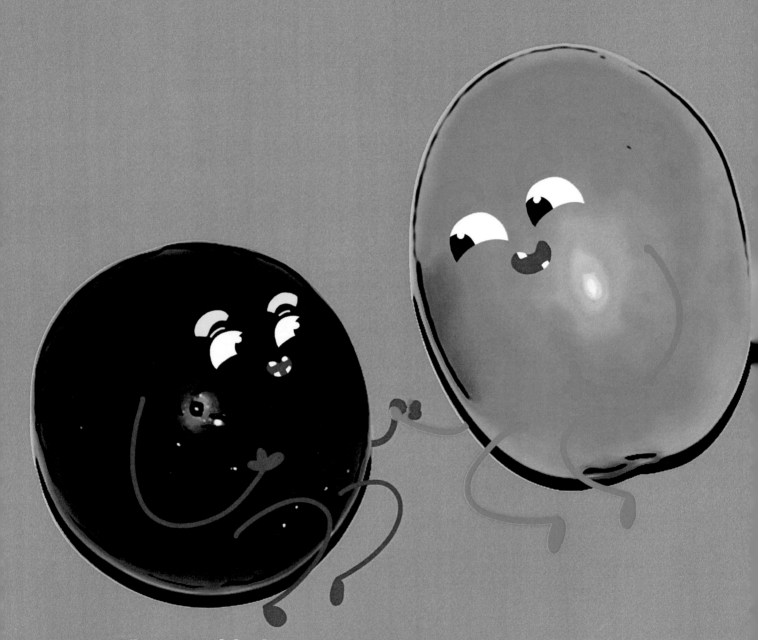

They nodded agreement those fruit of the vine.
Compared to that half popped guy they were fine!

Kenny was mad at the two sour grapes.
"They're lucky to be in a bunch for Pete's sake!
And I'm all alone 'cause there's no one like me...
a half popped kernel is not easy to be."

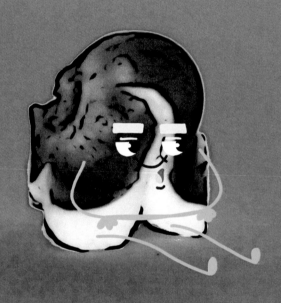

When Kenny moved on to the pantry he saw
a split open cookie some might say had a flaw...

All the cream was on one half, the other half bare,
and the side left with nothing thought that wasn't fair.
"What is the chocolate without all the cream?
We are supposed to be on the same team!"

"You're still made of chocolate," Kenny chimed in, "and you two can smoosh back together again."

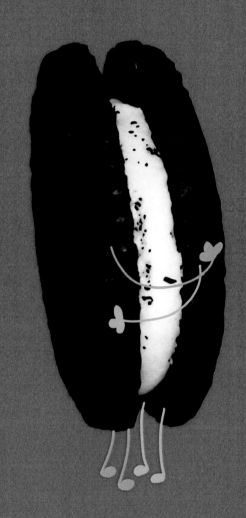

With a shrug and a hug, the cookie complied.
You'd never have guessed which had been the creamed side.

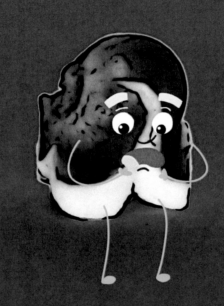

Then Kenny wondered, "How can it be?
How can anyone think they're worse off than me?"

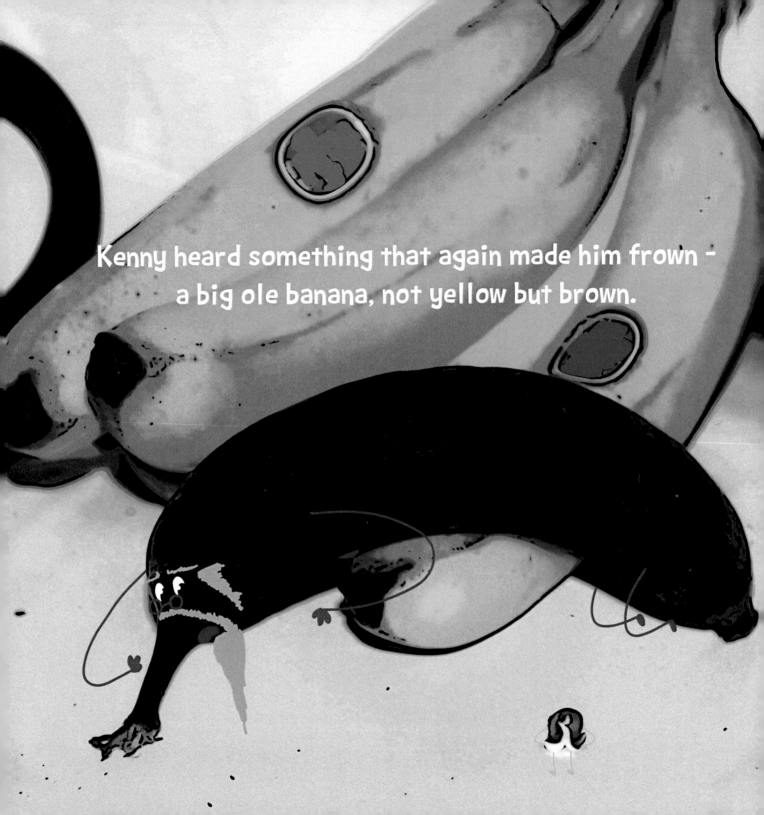

Kenny heard something that again made him frown –
a big ole banana, not yellow but brown.

"Oh there was a time I had such a peel
but now I look dark and I'm mushy to feel."
The forlorn banana was stuck in a rut.
He was down on his luck until Kenny piped up...

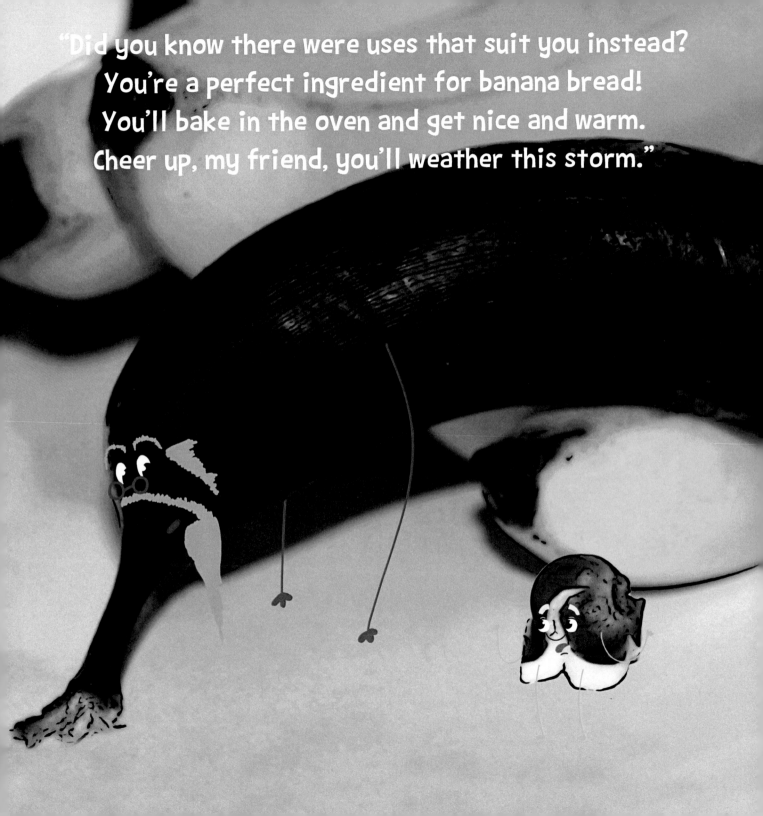

"Did you know there were uses that suit you instead?
You're a perfect ingredient for banana bread!
You'll bake in the oven and get nice and warm.
Cheer up, my friend, you'll weather this storm."

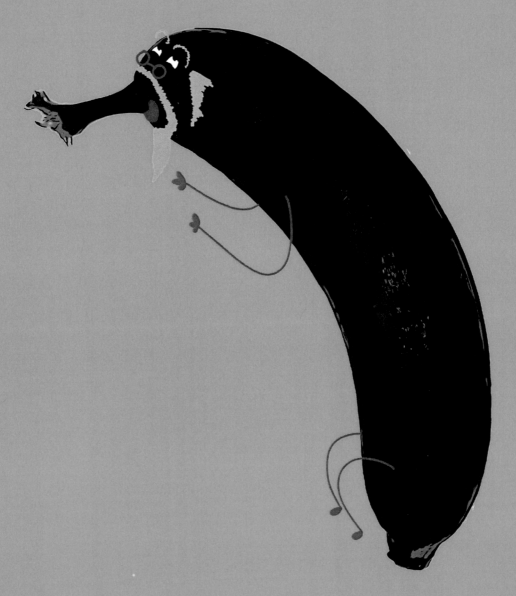

That made the brown banana less blue.
He started to look at the positives too!

And just when he thought that his work here was done,
a circular blur blew past in a run.
"Where are you going?" Kenny wanted to know.
"I'm out of this kitchen!" said a Cereal 'O.'

Kenny kept up with the cereal piece,
"Won't you be happy to be part of a feast?"
The whole-grain 'O' stopped and turned back south,
"But what if I get all the milk in my mouth?"

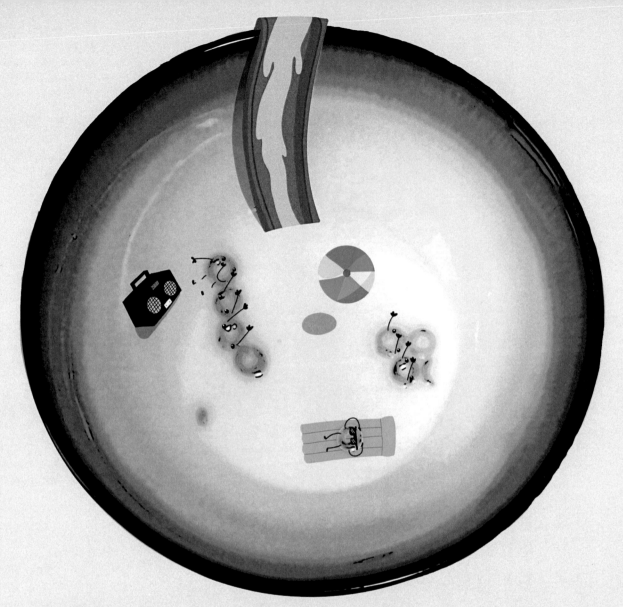

"Don't worry buddy you'll float to the top.
You can lie on your back and the fun won't stop!
You'll be with your friends and slurped from a spoon...
you'll be part of a well balanced breakfast real soon."

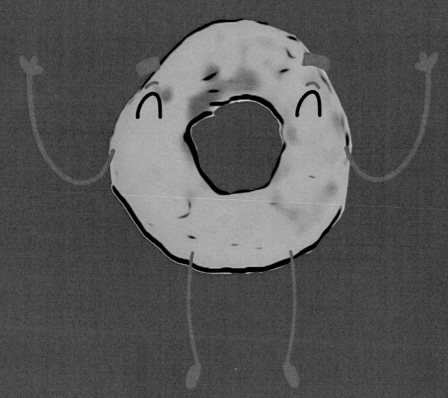

The tiny 'O' smiled and turned back around,
thrilled with this new information he'd found.

But that just left Kenny alone once again
to return to the empty bowl and what then?

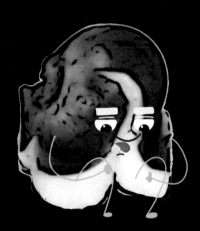

He couldn't do much about his small size.

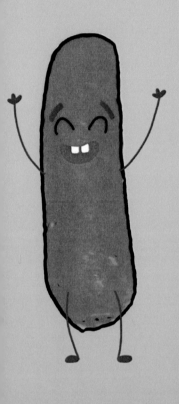

His color was bland to everyone's eyes.

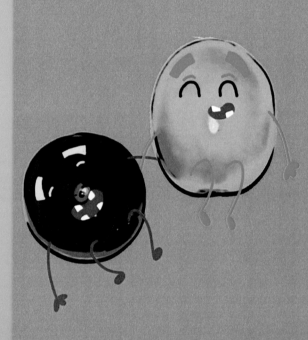

He had no one to pair with to make himself whole.

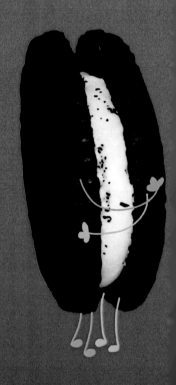

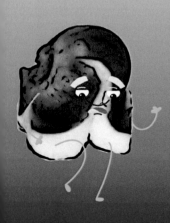

No baked goods were made from a poor half popped soul.

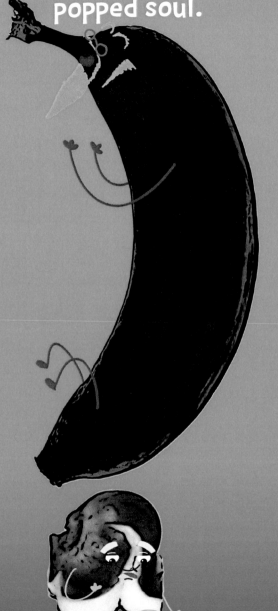

He'd sink to the bottom of a bowl full of milk. His uniqueness kept him apart from his ilk.

Kenny gave up and went back to his bowl,
cheering up others had taken its toll.
So Kenny the Kernel who was only half
popped, who turned out that way when
the microwave stopped,
was ready to call the whole thing quits...

when he was suddenly grabbed by some fingertips!

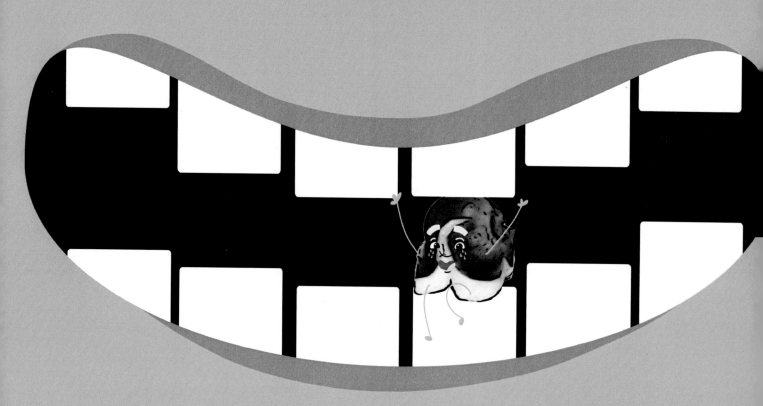

With a smile of shock and a teardrop of joy
Kenny finally felt like the golden boy.
He smiled all the way through crunch after crunch,
believing, at last, he was worthy to munch.